Ogopogo Odyssey

Written by D.A. Hawes

Illustrated by Maggie Parr

PROMONTORY
PRESS

Ogopogo Odyssey

Promontory Press Inc.
www.promontorypress.com

ISBN 978-1-927559-74-1

Printed in Canada
Cover and illustrations by Maggie Parr

098765432

Thanks to my family, Mark, Ashley, Colin & Jenny for always believing in the Ogopogo and in me. Thanks also to Maggie for sharing my dream and bringing this story to life through her wonderful illustrations.

D.A. Hawes

Author's Note

Many people believe that the creature described in this story really exists. Ogopogo or *N'ha-a-itk**, as the Okanagan Syilx People (Okanagan Nation Alliance) call him, has been the subject of much controversy over the past two centuries. Even though the first recorded sighting wasn't until 1872, there are many native legends dating even further back that refer to the "monster" which inhabits Okanagan Lake. The story of Chief Timbasket's demise, as told by the First Nations woman in this story, is based on local folklore. The Ogopogo continues to be a mascot for many tourist attractions in the Okanagan Valley. Every year there are at least five or six sightings of Ogopogo and many scientists are certain that such lake creatures really do exist.

*The traditional word is actually spelled Nha-ha-it-kw

Colin raised his sword against Blackbeard and his band of nasty pirates when it happened.

Just as he lunged for the pirate king, Colin spotted something strange parting the waters of the lake.

His world of make-believe melted away. His soldiers retreated into the blazing sands of the beach, the pirates ran off with chests of gold, and the mermaids swam back to their underwater kingdom. In an instant, Colin knew that the creature heading across Okanagan Lake was the famous lake monster known as the Ogopogo.

But when he looked again, Colin could only see the rise and fall of waves on the water. Where was the creature? Had the Ogopogo slipped beneath the water back to his underwater cave? Rubbing his eyes, Colin searched once more but he could only see ripples of water floating across the lake and hear the gentle sound of water lapping at the edge of the pier.

Colin had already heard all about the Ogopogo. On the day he had arrived for his summer vacation, it was Grandpa who took him through the vineyard and down to the lake, all the while telling him stories of the Ogopogo. This lake creature was famous and it seemed that every shop in town had T-shirts, mugs, and posters with a gigantic but very friendly looking Ogopogo. Even the shop in his grandparents' vineyard sold postcards showing the smiling creature welcoming tourists to the Okanagan Valley.

With a giant leap, Colin flew off the pier and raced across the sand, which was as hot as firecrackers between his toes. Racing through his grandfather's vineyard, he reached the back porch of his grandparents' house, flew up the steps two at a time, and burst through the door.

"I think I saw him! The Ogopogo! Right here—just off the pier! I was playing pirates and suddenly I saw him move out on the water!"

Colin's eyes darted back and forth between his grandparents. He was certain they would be as excited as he was.

But Grandma just smiled, ruffled his hair, and said, "You are so much like your mother. What an imagination! She used to lead us on with stories like that too!"

Grandpa chuckled. "Sounds like we need to get out my biggest fishing rod. You know, a few years back, they even offered a million-dollar reward to anyone who could catch the Ogopogo." He lowered his voice to a whisper. "Just think of what we could do with a million bucks."

Then Grandpa winked, picked up his hat, and headed out to the vineyard. They hadn't believed a word Colin had said.

Crushed, Colin wandered back through the vineyard, the sweet smell of grapes filling the air, as the workers scurried around preparing for the harvest. When he reached the pier, the lake was calm and flat. His eyes scanned the lake but it was as if nothing had ever happened.

Over the next few days, Colin couldn't get the Ogopogo out of his mind. When he slept, the creature surfaced in his dreams. It rose again from the warm, blue waters of the lake. He dreamed that he was riding the Ogopogo from one end of the lake to the other.

When his mom phoned a few days later, Colin was tempted to ask her about the Ogopogo but he was sure she would tease him just like Grandma and Grandpa had done.

"Yes, Mom. I'm having a great time," he told her, but he said nothing about the mysterious creature.

Somehow, playing pirates and hunting for buried treasure were never quite the same after that. On the beach Colin spent most of his time gazing out at the lake, hoping to catch a glimpse of the Ogopogo.

Sometimes he thought he saw the creature, but then he would realize it was only a wave made by a passing boat. Colin began to wonder if he'd imagined those ripples on the water.

Perhaps he would never see the Ogopogo again.

One day, while scooping sand into his bucket on the beach, Colin felt a shadow cool and dark across his back. He turned and looked up into the big brown eyes of a stranger.

When the native woman finally spoke, her voice was as rough and raspy as the sandpaper Grandpa scraped across the wood in his workshop.

"You've seen him, haven't you?" It was a statement, not a question. Colin thought she looked as old as forever.

"Seen who?" Colin finally replied.

"The Ogopogo. You've seen him, I know. Once you've seen him, it never goes away."

"What never goes away?"

"The look in your eyes that tells me you've seen him."

How could she have known? The caw-caw of a raven overhead sent a shiver down Colin's spine as he eyed this mysterious stranger.

"Have you seen him?" he asked.

"Just once, but that was many years ago now."

She motioned for Colin to join her as she sat down in the soft sand. At first she was silent, her eyes brooding over the water as it lapped against the beach. Finally she spoke.

"Do you wish to know more about this Ogopogo, as you call him?"

"I sure do!" Colin replied.

"My ancestors called him *N'ha-a-itk*, the sacred creature of the lake. Nowadays, he is known as the Ogopogo. His home is many miles down the lake in an underwater cave near Rattlesnake Island. He roams the waters of the entire lake. These waters are his playground."

Colin was eager to know more. At last, someone who would talk about the Ogopogo.

"How long has he lived here? Is he dangerous? How can I see him again?"

"One question at a time," she advised. A crooked smile broke through the brown wrinkles of her face.

Then she continued. "*N'ha-a-itk*, or as you say, Ogopogo, is a gentle creature unless he is angry. He demands the respect of those who cross his waters. In the old days, it was the custom to offer sacrifices to *N'ha-a-itk* as the people would paddle their canoes across his waters. Sometimes it would be a chicken or a pig."

Colin giggled as he imagined the Ogopogo swallowing a chicken with its feathers flying.

"Now one day," she continued, "a visiting Chief named Timbasket dared to challenge the great serpent of the lake. Scoffing at the warnings given to him by local bands, Chief Timbasket refused to bring along a sacrifice."

"What happened?" Colin was eager to hear more.

"He got into his canoe and paddled close to *N'ha-a-itk's* cave, bringing no offering for the mighty creature. In one swift movement, *N'ha-a-itk* rose to the surface and swallowed both Timbasket and his canoe. Not a trace of the Chief or his canoe was ever found."

Colin scanned the lake as if expecting to see the remains of Chief Timbasket's canoe. The old woman's story seemed so real.

"Do they still throw chickens and pigs to the Ogopogo?" Colin asked.

"Oh, no! But even now it is still important to show him respect. I knew that you would understand because you have seen him and you believe."

"My grandparents think I imagined it." Colin couldn't disguise his disappointment.

"Most people are skeptics. Don't let it worry you. Now, I must go."

And with that, the native woman lifted herself from the sand.

"Don't ever forget," she said, and then turned and walked down the beach.

"I won't!" Colin called back.

He watched her until she disappeared from sight. And then, he whispered, "I'll never forget—not ever."

When his mother arrived several days later to take him home, Colin couldn't wait to tell her all about his summer.

"Look at how tanned you are!" she exclaimed. "I can see that you've been spending your time at the beach." She hugged him tightly and loaded his bags into the car.

Colin looked back toward his grandparents' vineyard, the lake shimmering and blue in the background. As he waved to his grandparents, he wondered when he would see the Ogopogo again.

His mother's eyes gazed into his own as she said, "You've seen him, haven't you?"

"How did you know?" Colin asked, astounded.

"By the look in your eyes," she whispered. "And believe me, I should know. I've seen him too."

Colin's eyes widened and a smile broke across his face. He knew he would meet the Ogopogo again.

"See you next summer!" he yelled to his grandparents as the car pulled out of the driveway.

His eyes took one last glance over Okanagan Lake. And then, in an instant, several ripples appeared and a series of green humps rose from the water.

Colin's eyes widened and his heart pounded.
It was the Ogopogo!

When he looked again, the creature had vanished.

Taking one last look at Grandpa's vineyard with the lake glistening in the background, Colin whispered, "See you next summer, too."